Best Stories for Eight-Year-Olds

Enid Blyton
Pictures by Thomas Taylor

BLOOMSBURY
CHILDREN'S
BOOKS

Enid Blyton titles available at Bloomsbury
Children's Books

Adventure!
Mischief at St Rollo's
The Children of Kidillin
The Secret of Cliff Castle
Smuggler Ben
The Boy Who Wanted a Dog
The Adventure of the Secret Necklace

Happy Days!
The Adventures of Mr Pink-Whistle
Run-About's Holiday
Bimbo and Topsy
Hello Mr Twiddle
Shuffle the Shoemaker
Mr Meddle's Mischief
Snowball the Pony
The Adventures of Binkle and Flip

Enid Blyton Age-Ranged Story Collections
Best Stories for Five-Year-Olds
Best Stories for Six-Year-Olds
Best Stories for Seven-Year-Olds

Best Stories for
Eight-Year-Olds

Best Stories for Eight-Year-Olds
First Published by Bloomsbury Publishing Plc in 1997
36 Soho Square, London W1D 3QY

Enid Blyton

Copyright © Text Enid Blyton Limited
Copyright © Illustrations Thomas Taylor 1997

The moral right of the author and illustrator has been asserted
A CIP catalogue record of this book is available from the British Library

ISBN 978 0 7475 3228 6

All papers used by Bloomsbury Publishing are natural, recyclable products made from wood grown in well-managed forests. The manufacturing processes conform to the environmental regulations of the country of origin.

Printed in India by Gopsons Papers Ltd, Noida

13 15 17 19 20 18 16 14 12

Cover design Mandy Sherliker

Contents

Dear Children

Enid Blyton was my mother and when I came home from school, I would eagerly read the pages of the story she had written that day. If she was writing a long book I had to wait for several days to find out how it was going to end. It was no use asking my mother how it ended, because she didn't know until she wrote the last chapter!

Enid Blyton loved animals and so she wrote many stories about them. When she was a little girl she wasn't allowed to have any pets because her parents thought an animal would mess up the house and garden.

One day she found a little lost kitten and took it home. She didn't tell anyone and kept it hidden in a shed where she looked after it lovingly. She came home from school two weeks later to find her kitten gone. Her mother had found it and given it away to someone else. So when Enid Blyton wrote a story like The Clever White Kitten, she understood exactly how Elsie felt about the silver kitten.

When Enid Blyton had her own home, she kept dogs, cats, doves, pigeons, goldfish, a tortoise and hens. I loved having so many creatures around me and I was even allowed to keep pet mice!

I hope you'll enjoy these stories. Try reading them to your younger brothers and sisters, you'll find it fun to share them.

With love from
Gillian

THE GRANDPA CLOCK

The Grandpa clock stood up on the landing all day and night, ticking solemnly away by himself. He was a very tall clock, much, much taller than the children, and he was really a grandfather clock, of course – but everyone called him Grandpa because he was so nice.

He didn't like being up on the bedroom landing. He wanted to be down in the hall, and see a bit of life. He wasn't even on the *front* landing – he was on the back one, where the boxroom and the guest room were, so he didn't really see much of anything that went on in the house.

'I wish I was down in the hall!' he thought, whenever he heard someone ringing the bell or knocking at the door. 'I wonder who that is? Why can't I be down there and see? And I wish I could go and visit the kitchen. So many people come there. I can hear their voices. The cat goes there a lot too, and I like her.'

But it wasn't a bit of good, the back landing was his place and there he had to stay. Then one day something exciting happened – and things were suddenly quite different!

It happened one night that a small imp called Scuttle-About lost his way in the dark, and climbed in at the landing window to take shelter. He heard the tick-tock, tock-tock of the Grandpa clock, and he ran to it.

'May I creep inside you?' he whispered. 'Will you hide me, Grandpa Clock?'

'Yes! I've a door under my big face. Open it and climb inside,' said Grandpa. 'Be careful of my pendulum that swings to and fro. It might hit you.'

The imp was very careful. He crouched down below the pendulum and felt it scrape the top of his head as it swung to and fro. Tick-tock, tick-tock!

He took off his Scuttle-About shoes. They were very magic and he could run about, fast as a hare in them – but his feet were tired now and he wanted to curl up and rest for the night.

Soon he was fast asleep and snoring a little. Grandpa ticked steadily all the time, feeling most excited to have a little imp asleep just under his pendulum!

'Tick-tock! It's time to be up! Tick-tock! You must hurry away!' ticked old Grandpa, when he heard the birds beginning to sing outside. He knew that Annie the cook would soon be up and about. He didn't want her to see the imp when he ran off again.

Scuttle-About woke up with a jump. He stretched himself and hit the swinging pendulum with his hand.

'Hey, don't do that!' said Grandpa. 'You'll make me go slow! Hurry – I believe I can hear someone coming.'

The imp swung open the door and fled in a fright. Grandpa never saw him again. But Scuttle-About left something behind him – he left his little magic shoes!

And soon the magic in them spread to the old Grandpa clock. He suddenly felt restless. He ticked a little faster. And then, to his enormous surprise, he gave a little jiggety-jig, rocking to and fro as he ticked.

'Strange! I seem to be able to move!' said Grandpa, astonished. 'I'm sure I moved an inch or two then. There! I did it again. Good gracious – I've moved out from the wall!'

It was the Scuttle-About spell in the little shoes working, of course. But Grandpa didn't know that. He just thought that for some strange reason he could move about.

Move about! Why, he had always longed to do that. He had always wanted to go into the hall and into the kitchen. Supposing he could? Just suppose he could get himself downstairs – how exciting that would be!

Well, it was difficult for him to move at first, but he soon got used to it. He could only move by rocking himself, or doing a curious little jump that made him tick very fast indeed as if he were quite out of breath.

It took him about half an hour to reach the front landing. Even that was exciting to him

because it was years since he had seen it. There were flowers there, and a big chair, and a chest. Grandpa ticked away to them in a loud voice.

'I'm going downstairs when I've got my breath! I'm going exploring!'

But he didn't get downstairs because at that moment the children's father came out of his room to go and wake the children. He almost bumped into Grandpa, who was just outside his bedroom door.

'Good gracious! It's the Grandpa clock!' he said. 'However did it get here? Has someone been having a joke?'

Poor Grandpa! He was carried straight back to his own place on the back landing. He was bitterly disappointed. He grumbled away to himself, ticking very crossly.

'Tick-tock, what a nasty shock, for a poor old clock!' he ticked.

The children soon heard that he had been found outside their father's door and they came to stare at him. 'Who put you there? Grandpa,

don't you start wandering about at night!' they said.

Well, the Grandpa clock wasn't going to stop his bit of travelling if he could help it! Somehow or other he was going to get downstairs! Surely, if the family found him in the hall they would let him stay there? Wasn't that the proper place for a big grandfather clock?

That afternoon, when the children were at school and their mother was resting, the clock felt that it couldn't keep still on the dull dark landing any longer. He must at least go to the top of the stairs and look down.

So he went to the top of the stairs, rocking himself slowly along, sometimes giving a funny little jump. He couldn't help feeling very excited.

The stairs looked very long and very steep. It wasn't much good thinking of rocking himself down them. He would have to do little jumps down from one stair to the next. So down he went – jump – jump – jump – hop – hop!

It was very dangerous. He nearly missed a stair once or twice, and shivered in fright. But at last he was at the bottom, standing in the hall. How wonderful!

The hall seemed a most exciting place. There were mats and chairs, umbrellas, walking sticks and a little table with flowers on it. Now, where could the clock put himself so that he could see the people who came to the door? He badly wanted to have a bit of company.

The cat had heard the noise Grandpa made coming downstairs, and she came out of the kitchen to see what it was. She was amazed to see the Grandpa clock standing by the hall table! She went up and sniffed at him. The sniffing tickled Grandpa, and made him jump.

That frightened the cat. She put her tail in the air and fled to the kitchen. The clock heard voices coming from there.

'I must go there and listen,' he thought so he rocked and hopped to the kitchen door. The cook was out in the scullery talking to the milkman and the baker. Grandpa rocked inside and stood by the cupboard. My, what a thrilling place the kitchen was – and look at that lovely red fire! Grandpa began to wish he lived in the kitchen.

The cook came back. She saw Grandpa at once and gave a scream. 'Milkman! Baker! Help, help! Here's old Grandpa in the kitchen!'

They came rushing in, expecting to see an old man. Cook pointed to the clock. 'There, look! How did he get there? Oh, oh, I feel faint!'

The Grandpa clock was scared. When the milkman and the baker helped the cook to a chair, he rocked himself out of the kitchen and put himself back in the hall. He stood there, feeling very excited. My word, this was life!

The children's mother came running down the stairs. She suddenly saw Grandpa by the hall table, and stopped in amazement.

'Cook!' she called. 'Who put old Grandpa down in the hall?'

'Oh, Mam! Do you mean to say he's out there now?' cried the cook, looking into the hall. 'He was standing in the kitchen a minute ago!'

'Oh, nonsense!' said her mistress. 'But *how* did he get into the hall? Help me upstairs with him, Cook. This is most extraordinary.

The children were surprised to hear what had happened when they came home. First, the cook told them how Grandpa had appeared in the kitchen, then their mother told them how she had seen him in the hall.

'Perhaps old Grandpa is dull and bored, living up on the back landing, where nothing happens and nobody goes,' said Mary. 'Can't we let him live in the hall? He's so nice.'

But back on the landing he had to go. He was really most annoyed. Now he would have to hop all the way downstairs again if he wanted to stand in hall.

'I'll wait till night comes and everyone is in bed,' he thought, ticking solemnly on the landing. 'Then I'll go down again, and look into all the rooms. That will be most exciting.'

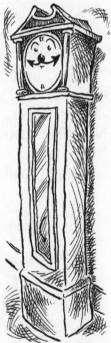

So that night, when it was quite dark and everyone was asleep, old Grandpa thought he would go downstairs once more. And just as he was thinking about this he heard a little noise downstairs. Who was it? The cat wandering about? Or mice playing? Perhaps it was that imp coming back again.

Grandpa decided to go and see. So off he went, rocking himself to the top of the stairs.

He stood at the top, and heard a noise again. The noise wasn't the cat, or the mice, or the imp. It was a burglar! He had forced his way into the house and was in the hall. Think of that!

Grandpa hopped down the first stair. Then he hopped down the next one – but alas, he missed it! With a really tremendous noise he slid and slithered all the way from the top to the bottom, and landed on top of the alarmed burglar. He was knocked over like a skittle, and lay on the carpet, quite still.

Then things happened quickly. Doors flew open, lights went on, voices called out. 'What was that noise, what's happening?' And down the stairs poured the whole family.

'Why, my goodness me, here's a man lying flat on the floor and the old Grandpa clock on

top of him!' said the children's father, in astonishment. 'Ring up the police, quickly!'

The police came. They took the burglar away. One of them nodded at the old clock, which had now been stood upright in the hall, and was watching everything in the greatest excitement.

'What was your clock doing, knocking a burglar down in the middle of the night?' he said. 'Good thing you had him in the hall!'

'Well, we didn't. He lives on the back landing,' said Mary. 'But, oh – do, do let him live downstairs in the hall, Daddy, will you? I'm sure he wants to! I'm sure he was coming downstairs and he slipped and fell on top of the burglar. He deserves a reward, Daddy, he really does!'

So now old Grandpa lives downstairs, and loves it. And nobody has discovered to this day that he has a tiny pair of Scuttle-About shoes

inside his case! It will be sad if somebody takes them out, won't it? He won't ever be able to wander into the kitchen again at night and talk to the cat.

Tick-tock, tick-tock. I believe I can hear him coming!

THE TIGER AND
THE RABBIT

As the splendid tiger was wandering through the jungle one day a little sandy rabbit hopped out of a hole in front of him. The rabbit was so terrified at seeing the great tiger near at hand that he sat there unable to move.

The tiger put his great paw down on the rabbit and held him.

'Mercy, mercy!' squealed the rabbit. 'Let me free, great tiger! Oh, mercy mercy! If you will let me go I will repay you one day!'

'Ho!' said the tiger scornfully. 'How can a poor creature like you do a good turn to a tiger?'

'I might save your life, Master!' cried the rabbit eagerly. 'You cannot tell. Oh, great and excellent tiger, braver and stronger than King Lion himself, let me go! I will save your life some day, that I promise you! You have only to roar for me and I will come from my burrow like the wind!'

'Well,' said the tiger, taking his big paw from the trembling rabbit, 'you may go! I have had my dinner, and do not need a small mouthful like you. I will see if you keep your word – but you rabbits are poor creatures, timid and foolish. You couldn't help a mouse, and as for a tiger – well – it is almost impertinent to think of such a thing!'

The rabbit did not wait for a moment, fearful lest the tiger should change his mind and gobble him up. He darted into his burrow and sat there shivering, thinking over and over again of what a narrow escape he had had. His heart was full of gratitude to the merciful tiger, and he longed to show him some kindness in return.

The tiger forgot all about the rabbit. He hunted throughout the week, and ate well. He slept in a close thicket of trees and bushes during the hot daytime, and sometimes was so well fed that he slept half the night as well.

He stole cattle from a native village. First one fat cow he took and then another. The natives were angry and afraid. They made up their minds to set a trap for the tiger. They found the path he used each night to the cattle enclosure, and in the middle of that they dug a very deep pit.

It was wide as well as deep. Then, to prevent the tiger from scraping a foothold in the walls to spring out of the pit, they rammed the cut trunks of trees closely together all around the pit. On the top they placed a loose platform of sticks, laid across from side to side, and covered with leaves and grass to look as if it were part of the path.

'Ha!' said the natives, pleased with their work. 'This is a fine trap! Once the tiger treads on the top of it he will fall down into the pit with a crash. It is too deep for him to leap out of, and because it is lined with timbers he cannot scrape footholds in the sides! We shall catch him tonight.'

They were right! The tiger came padding along that night, and when he trod on the loose platform of leaves and sticks it gave way beneath his weight and he fell with a crash into the pit.

How angry he was! How he roared! How he

scraped at the timbers lining the pit – but they were too well placed to give way. The tiger was caught. He could not jump out for the pit was too deep. There he must stay until the natives came the next morning and killed him with spears.

The tiger would not lie still. He paced round and round the great pit, and every now and again he lifted his great head and roared into the night. The natives shook to hear him. Someone else heard him too – the little rabbit whose life he had spared.

'It is my friend the tiger asking for me!' cried the rabbit, and he set off at top speed to the pit. When he reached it he peered down at the furious tiger.

'Friend!' he cried. 'I come to help you!'

The tiger looked at him in scorn.

'Ho, the foolish rabbit again! Well, rabbit, and how are you going to get me out of this? Ah, for all your grand promises, you are nothing but a silly, timid little creature, of no use to a royal beast like myself! Go away and leave me to myself.'

The rabbit hopped down fearlessly into the pit and looked all round it. He saw the timbers rammed tightly against the wall, and as his bright eyes roved round, an idea came into his head.

'Sir!' he said to the tiger. 'Master! I can set you free! I will get my friends to help me. Do not despair!'

To the tiger's great surprise the rabbit hopped up the side of the pit and disappeared into the night.

But he was soon back again, this time with about fifty rabbits like himself, all rather

scared, but determined to do what their friend asked them.

The rabbit made ten hop down into the pit with him, the tiger first promising that he would not hurt any of them. The rest began to burrow swiftly outside the pit, down, down, down into the earth.

The tiger watched the rabbits inside the pit scornfully. He had no faith in such silly creatures! What were they going to do? If *he* could not get out of the pit with all his strength, surely they did not think *they* could get him out!

The rabbits inside the pit began to gnaw hard at one of the tree trunks. Their sharp teeth bit right through the bark, right into the heart of the tree. Gnaw, gnaw, gnaw! How they bit into the timber, and very soon the tiger saw that they had bitten the trunk right in half. Then they set to work on the same tree trunk but a good bit lower down. Soon they had taken out a large piece from the trunk and it fell to the bottom of the pit with a crash. Then they set to work on the next piece of timber.

When they had bitten big pieces out of five pieces of timber the tiger heard a curious scraping sound on the other side of the pit wall. It was all the other rabbits burrowing nearer and nearer to the pit! They had dug an enormous hole, working hard with their strong

feet, and had tunnelled downwards to the side of the pit – just to where the inside rabbits had bitten out the pieces of tree trunks! Soon they made a hole right into the pit itself, and crawled through the space left where the tree trunks had been bitten through.

'Now, Master,' said the rabbit in excitement, 'can you crawl into this space in the pit wall between the timber we have bitten, and escape through the big tunnel we have made?'

Of course he could! It didn't take a moment for the tiger to squeeze through and make his way up the big tunnel that all the rabbits had made for him. Soon he stood in the open air again, glad to be free. 'Good night, Master!' called the rabbit. 'I said I would repay you for your mercy to me! I have done so!'

Off they went to their burrows, and the tiger bounded gladly away to the jungle. As for the natives next day when they came to the pit, how amazed they were to find the timbers that lined the pit bitten through, and a great tunnel leading out of it.

'It was no tiger we caught!' they cried. 'It must have been a MONSTROUS rabbit!'

THE SECRET CAVE

The adventure of the Secret Cave really began on the day when we all went out on the cliff to fly our new kite. I am Roger, and Joan and William are my sister and brother. William's the eldest, and Joan and I are twins.

We live in a house near the sea, but it is very lonely because there is no other house anywhere near us, except the big house on the cliff, and that is empty. We often wished it was full of children so that we could play with them, but as it wasn't we had to be content to play by ourselves.

Mummy and Daddy were going away for a month on a sea trip, and they were leaving that very day. We were all feeling very sad about it, because home is a funny sort of place without Mummy. But it was holiday time, and our governess had gone, so there was only old Sarah to look after us, and we thought we'd have quite a good time really.

Mummy gave us a glorious new kite just as she said goodbye, and told us to go and fly it as soon as they had gone; then we shouldn't feel so bad about everything. So when the car had disappeared down the hill, we took our new kite and went out on the windy cliff.

William soon got it up in the air, and it flew like a bird. But suddenly the wind dropped and the kite gave a great dip downwards. William pulled hard at it, but it wasn't any good. Down and down it went, and at last disappeared behind some trees.

'Bother!' we said. 'Let's go and look for it.'

We raced over the cliff till we came to the clump of stunted trees behind which our kite had gone. Then we found that the string disappeared over the high wall that surrounded the big house on the cliff.

'The kite must have fallen in the garden,' said William. 'What shall we do?'

'Go and knock at the front door and ask for it,' said Joan. 'There might be a caretaker there.'

So we ran round to the front gate and went up the long drive. We soon came to the front door. It was a big wooden one with a large knocker. William knocked hard and we heard the sound go echoing through the house.

Nobody came, so we each of us knocked in turn, very loudly indeed. After we had waited for about five minutes without anyone opening the door, we decided that the house must be quite empty, without a caretaker or anyone at all.

'Well, how are we to get our kite?' I asked.

'The only thing to do is to climb over the wall,' said William. 'We can't ask anyone's permission because there isn't anyone to ask. Come on. We can't lose our lovely kite.'

So we ran down the drive again and made our way to the back of the garden wall, which stood high above our heads. William managed to climb up it first, and then jumped down on the other side.

'Come on, you others,' he called. 'It's all right. Oh, wait a minute, though. I've got an idea. Stand away from the wall, both of you. I've found a box here, and I'm going to throw it over. You can stand on it, and then you will easily be able to climb up the wall.'

William threw over the box. Then we stood on it and just managed to reach the top. We jumped down, and there we all were in the deserted garden of the house on the cliff.

It was a very wild place, for no one had bothered about it for years. Everything was overgrown, and the paths were covered with green moss that was like velvet to walk on. I don't know why, but we felt at first as if we ought to talk in whispers.

'Where's our kite?' said Joan. 'Look, William, there's the string. Let's follow it and we shall soon find the kite.'

So we followed the string, and it led us over a stretch of long grass that had once been a big lawn, down a thick shrubbery, and past some greenhouses whose glass was all broken.

Then William gave a shout.

'There it is!' he said, and he pointed to where a little shed stood hidden away in a dark corner. We all looked at it, and, sure enough, there was the kite perched up on the roof. It didn't take us long to pull it down, and we found that one of the sticks that ran across it was broken, so we couldn't fly it any more that day. We were sorry about that, and we wondered what we should do for the rest of the morning.

'Why can't we stay here and explore the garden?' asked Joan. 'We shouldn't do any harm, and it would be great fun.'

'All right, we will,' said William, who always decides everything because he is the eldest.

So we began exploring, and it really was fun. Then it suddenly began to rain, and as none of us had our mackintoshes with us we got wet.

'We must shelter somewhere,' said William. 'Sarah will be very cross if we go home soaked through.'

'Well, what about that little shed, where we found the kite?' I asked. 'That would do nicely.'

So we raced to the shed, but the door was locked, so we couldn't get in.

'How about a window?' cried Joan. 'Here's one with the latch broken. Push it, William. Oh, good, it's open and we can climb in. What an adventure we're having!'

We all climbed in. I went to the door, and what do you think? The key was *inside*!

'Well, if that isn't a curious thing,' said William, looking at it. 'If you lock a door from the inside you usually lock yourself in too. But there's nobody here. It's a mystery!'

But we soon forgot about the key in our excitement over the shed. It really was a lovely little place. There was a funny old chair with a crooked leg that William felt sure he could mend if he had his tools. There was a battered old table in one corner, and two small stools, one with a leg off. Along one side of the shed was a shelf, very dusty and dirty.

'I say! Wouldn't this shed make a perfectly lovely little house for us to play in on rainy days?' William suddenly said. 'We could clean it up and mend the stool and chair.'

'Oh, William, do let's!' said Joan, clapping her hands in delight. 'I've got some pretty orange stuff Mummy gave me, and I can make it into little curtains for the two windows. We can bring a pail and a scrubbing brush and clean the whole place up beautifully.'

'And we can use the shelf for storing things on,' I said. 'We can bring apples and biscuits here, and some of our books to read. Oh, what fun! But we must keep it a secret, or perhaps Sarah would stop us.'

'Well, we mustn't do any harm anywhere,' said William. 'After all, it isn't *our* shed, but I'm sure if the man who owns it, whoever he is, knew that we were going to clean it up and make it nice, he would only be too glad to let us. Now the rain's stopped – we must run home or we shall be late for dinner.'

We took our broken kite and raced home. We didn't need to climb over the wall again, because we found a dear little door in the wall with the key inside. So we opened the door, slipped out, locked it again, and William took the key away in his pocket in case tramps found it.

We were so excited at dinner time that Sarah got cross with us and threatened to send us to bed half an hour earlier if we didn't eat our food properly.

At last dinner was over and we ran out into our own garden to decide what we should take to the house on the cliff.

'Let's borrow the gardener's barrow,' said William. 'We can put heaps of things in that and wheel it easily.'

So we got the barrow and piled the things into it. Joan found the orange stuff and put that in, and popped her workbasket in too. I found a very old carpet that nobody used in the attic, and I put that in. William took his tools, and we went and asked Cook if she could give us anything to eat.

She was very nice, and gave us three slices of cake, a bottle of lemonade, and a bag of raisins. Then we had a great stroke of luck, because the gardener told us we could pick the apples off one of the trees and keep them for ourselves.

You can guess we had soon picked about fifty or sixty and put them into a basket. That went into the barrow too, and then it really was almost as much as we could manage to wheel it along.

'We can easily come back for our books and anything else we can think of,' said William. So off we went, all helping to push. At last we came to the little door in the wall and William unlocked it. We went through the garden until we came to our dear little shed.

'Oh, we ought to have brought something to clean it up with,' said Joan. 'Never mind, William. Empty these things out on to a newspaper in the corner, and we'll go back for a pail and a scrubbing brush and soap.'

Back we went, and at last after two or three more journeys we really had got everything we could think of that day. Then we had a lovely time cleaning up the shed. The floor was laid with big white flagstones, and they looked lovely when we had scrubbed them clean. We

washed the shelf and all the bits of furniture too, and soon the shed looked fine.

That was all we had time to do that day, but early the next morning we were back again, as you can guess. Joan made the little curtains and tied them back with a piece of old hair ribbon. They did look nice. William and I mended the stool and the chair and arranged the things we had brought.

Cook had given us half a jar of strawberry jam and a pot of honey, and we had bought some biscuits and nuts. Our books went up on the shelf, and the apples stood in a corner in their basket.

'Well, it really looks quite homey,' said Joan, jumping round the shed joyfully. 'What fun we shall have here. Don't my little curtains look nice, and isn't the carpet fine? Our feet would have been very cold on those bare flagstones.'

Well, I can't tell you how we enjoyed our time in that little shed. Every day that it rained we went there, and as it was a very wet summer we spent most of our time there. We ate our biscuits and apples, read our books and did puzzles, and Sarah thought we were as good as gold, though she didn't know at all where we went every day. She thought we were down by the sea, I think.

But the most exciting part of our adventure hadn't come yet. I must tell you about it now.

We had been using the shed for about three weeks when William lost a sixpence. It rolled on to the floor and disappeared. We turned back the carpet to look for it.

'There's a flagstone here that seems rather loose,' said William. 'Perhaps the sixpence has gone down the crack.'

'It *is* loose!' said Joan. 'Why, I can almost lift it!'

'I believe we *could* lift it,' said William. We slipped a thin iron bar in one of the cracks, and then suddenly the stone rose up! It came quite easily, and stood upright, balanced on one side.

And where it had been was a big black hole, with stone steps leading downwards!

What do you think of that? We were all so astonished that we simply knelt there and stared and stared.

'Why, it's a secret passage!' said William at last. 'What about exploring it?'

'Do you think it's safe?' asked Joan.

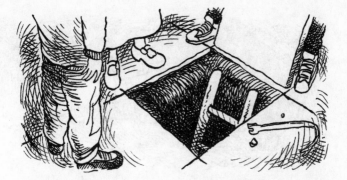

'Oh, I should think so,' said William. 'We can take our electric torches with us. This passage explains the key left inside the door. Someone must have gone to this shed, locked it from the inside, and then gone down the passage somewhere. It must lead out to some place or other. Oh, what an adventure!'

We got our torches from the shelf, and then, with William leading, we all climbed down the steps. They soon ended and we found ourselves in a narrow passage that led downwards fairly steeply.

'Do you know, I believe this passage leads to the seashore,' said William suddenly. 'I think it is going right through the cliff, and will come out to one of those rocky caves we have sometimes seen from a boat.'

And we found that William was right. For the passage, always sloping downwards, suddenly opened out into a small dark cave.

William couldn't see at first whether or not there was any way out of it besides the way we had come, and then he suddenly found it! It was just a small opening low down at one end, so small that a man would have found it quite difficult to squeeze through.

We squeezed through easily enough, of course, and then we found ourselves in a very big wide cave, lit by daylight. The thunder of breaking waves seemed very near, and as we made our way to the big opening where the daylight streamed through we saw the rough sea just outside it.

'You were right, William,' I said. 'That passage from our shed led right through the cliff down to this cave that is open to the sea. Look! When we stand on this ledge the waves almost reach our feet. I shouldn't be surprised if in very rough weather the sea washes right into the cave.'

'I don't think so,' said William, turning round to look. 'You see, the floor slopes upwards fairly steeply. Oh my! Just look there!'

We turned to see what he was exclaiming at, and what do you think? The floor of the cave was strewn with boxes of all sizes and shapes!

'Why, perhaps it's a smugglers' cave!' we cried. We rushed to the boxes, but all except two were fast locked. In the two unlocked ones were many clothes – very old-fashioned ones they were, too.

'Well, this *is* a find!' said William. 'I say, what about dressing up in these clothes and giving Sarah a surprise?'

We thought that would be lovely, so we quickly turned out the clothes and found some to fit us. Joan had a lovely frock right down to her ankles, and I had a funny little tunic sort of suit, and so did William. We put them on in the little shed because it was lighter there.

'Now, are we all ready?' said William. 'Well, come along then. We'll give Sarah the surprise of her life, and then we'll take her and the gardener to see our wonderful find.'

We danced through the door of the shed — and oh, my gracious goodness, didn't we get a shock?

Two gentlemen were walking up the moss-grown path by the shed! They saw us just at the same moment as we saw them, and we all stopped quite still and stared at one another.

One of the gentlemen looked as if he simply couldn't believe his eyes. He took off his glasses and cleaned them, and then he put them on again. But we were still there, and at last he spoke to us.

'Am I dreaming — or am I back in the days of long ago?' he said. 'Are you children of nowadays, or little long-ago ghosts?'

'We're quite real,' said William. 'We're only dressed up.'

'Well, that's a relief,' said the man. 'But what are you doing here? This garden belongs to my house.'

'Oh, are you the man who owns the house?' asked William.

'Yes,' he answered, 'and this gentleman is perhaps going to buy it from me. I'm too poor to keep it as it should be kept, you see. But you still haven't told me what you are doing here.'

Well, of course, we had to confess everything then. We told him how we had found the dear little shed by accident, and made it a sort of a home. And then we told him of our great find that afternoon.

'What!' he cried. 'Do you really mean to say you've found the secret passage to the cave? Why, it's been lost for years and years, and no one knew the secret. I lived here when I was a boy, but I never found it either, though I looked everywhere.'

Of course we had to show the way down to the cave, and when he saw the boxes lying there he turned so pale that Joan asked him if he was going to faint.

'No,' he said. 'But I'm going to tell you a little story, and you will understand then why I feel rather strange.'

And this is the story he told us.

'Many, many years ago,' he began, 'my family lived in France. There came a time when they were unjustly accused as traitors, and were forced to fly from the country. They packed up all their belongings and put them on board a ship to be brought to this country, where they had a house. This was the house. It had a secret passage from the shed to the sea, and the idea was to land at night with their belongings and go up through the passage unseen. They meant to live in the house until the trouble had blown over and they could go about here in safety, or return to France.'

'And did they?' asked William.

'No. Just as all the luggage had been safely put on board and the family were saying goodbye to their friends on shore, some men came galloping up and took them prisoners. The ship hurriedly put off without them and sailed safely to this place. The luggage was dumped down in this cave and the ship went back towards France. But, so the story goes, a storm came, and the whole crew were drowned. As for the family, some died in prison, and none of them ever came back to this house except one. He had been a small boy at the time and had no idea where the secret passage was, and though he searched everywhere he could not find it. So he gave it up and decided that all the family belongings were lost for ever.'

'And are these what he was looking for?' I asked.

'They are,' said the man. 'And, thanks to you, they are found again. Well, well, what an excitement! Now perhaps I shan't have to sell my own house. I might even be able to come and live here again with my family.'

'Have you got any children?' asked William.

'Yes, six,' said the man.

Well, we all gave a shout at that! Fancy having six children near to play with, when you've never had any at all! It seemed too good to be true.

But it *was* true! Mr Carnot, for that was the man's name, found that the boxes did contain all his old family treasures, and by selling some he had more than enough money to live at his old home once again with his family. I can tell you it was a most exciting day when they all arrived.

Daddy and Mummy could hardly believe all we had to tell them when they came home, but when Mr Carnot took them into our shed and down the passage to the cave, they soon knew it was true.

And now we have heaps of playmates. They are Billy, Anne, Marjorie, Jeanne, Laurence, and the baby. We often use the secret passage, and sometimes we even row to the cave in a boat, just like the sailors did all those many years ago.

TIDDLEY-POM'S PENCIL

Tiddley-Pom the tailor was very happy. The king had given him a beautiful gold pencil with his name on, because the little tailor had made him a splendid red party suit.

'Look!' Tiddley-Pom said to every one he met. 'Look! See my beautiful golden pencil. The king gave it to me!'

Tiddley-Pom's wife was very pleased. She took a good look at the pencil and said, 'Now, Tiddley-Pom, you just be careful with this pencil. You know how careless you are with your things – always putting them down here, there, and everywhere, and never being able to find them again. Just choose a safe place for your pencil, and keep it there when you are not using it.'

'In my pocket?' said Tiddley-Pom.

'No,' said his wife. 'That's a silly place,

47

because your pockets always have holes.'

'You should mend them,' said Tiddley-Pom.

'I do,' said Mrs Tiddley-Pom, 'but you will keep putting your scissors into them, Tiddley-Pom, and the points make holes.'

'I'll keep my pencil on the mantelpiece,' said Tiddley-Pom.

'No,' said his wife. 'It might roll off there.'

'Well,' said the tailor. 'I'll tie on a bit of string and tie the string to a button on my coat! What do you think of that, wife?'

'No good at all,' said Mrs Tiddley-Pom. 'You are always taking your coat off – and you forget where you leave it, so your pencil would be gone too! Do you know, Tiddley-Pom, that I found your coat on the *roof* the other day. Now how *did* it get there?'

'It must have been left there when I went up to watch the sweep's brush coming out of the chimney!' said the tailor going red. 'Oh, wife! I know such a good place! I'll keep my pencil behind my ear – like this!'

He stuck the lovely gold pencil behind his ear, and it stayed there nicely because Tiddley-Pom had great big pointed ears, and only the tip of the pencil could be seen sticking out.

'That's quite a good place,' said his wife. 'Now I'm going out shopping, Tiddley. So get on with your work whilst I'm gone.'

Off she went. Tiddley-Pom settled down to his sewing very happily, he whistled as he worked, and a good many of his friends came and chatted with him at the open window. One of them was old Dame Tubby, who had been away a week with her sister.

'I hear the king gave you a beautiful gold pencil, Tiddley-Pom,' she said. 'Will you show it to me?'

'Oh, haven't you seen it?' said the tailor. 'I'd love to show it to you.'

He put his hands into his pocket to get the pencil. It wasn't there.

'Funny!' said Tiddley-Pom. 'I usually keep my pencil there. Wait a minute. I may have put it on the mantelpiece.'

He ran to the mantelpiece. No pencil there either. Tiddley-Pom scratched his head and thought.

'It must be *somewhere* about!' he said. 'I had it about half an hour ago.'

'Perhaps it has been stolen,' said Dame Tubby.

'A valuable pencil like that might easily be stolen, you know. A witch or a gnome would be pleased to have it!'

'Ooh!' said Tiddley-Pom in alarm. 'So they might. Oh, Dame Tubby, Snippy the Gnome came in this morning – and Witch Toddles – and the Yellow Witch too – and Higgle the Gnome as well! Do you suppose any of them took it?'

'Well, I shouldn't think so,' said Dame Tubby. 'They are all friends of yours, aren't they? *I'll* tell you what to do, Tiddley-Pom. I've got a spell at home for robbers, I'll go and get it. Wait a minute. We'll soon get back your pencil!'

Dame Tubby ran off. On the way home she told every one about Tiddley-Pom's lost pencil, and how she was getting a spell to find the robber. So, before she had got back to the shop again, about twenty gnomes, goblins, witches, fairies, and pixies had arrived at Tiddley-Pom's, all anxious to hear the latest news of the wonderful pencil.

Dame Tubby came back, most important. In her hand she carried a little box. 'Look, Tiddley-Pom,' she said. 'There's a yellow powder in here. Blow it into the air and call upon it to find the one who has the pencil.'

'But how shall I know who has it?' asked Tiddley-Pom.

'Oh, you must choose something that the spell makes them do,' said Dame Tubby, excited. 'Tell the spell to start them braying like a donkey – or standing on their head – or galloping like a horse! Then as soon as the spell begins to work, we'll see which of us is doing that, and we'll find the pencil on him!'

'Ooh!' said Tiddley-Pom, 'it's a powerful spell. I know what I'll do. I'll tell it to make the robber quack like a duck and hop on one foot all the way down the street. Then we shall soon find the one who has my beautiful gold pencil.'

Tiddley-Pom took the box, and opened the lid. He blew the powder up into the air, crying, 'Spell, spell, find the one who has my pencil! Make him quack like a duck and hop all the way down the street!'

The powder flew up into the air with a queer crackling noise and disappeared.

Every one stood still and looked at every one else. Who was the thief? Nobody moved – and then, suddenly a most peculiar thing happened!

Tiddley-Pom began to quack! You should have head him!

'Quarck, quarck, quarck!' he said opening and shutting his mouth like a beak. 'Quarck, quarck, quarck, quarck!'

And then he put up one leg and began to hop

solemnly to the door – and out of it – and down the street! All the time he quacked very loudly; it did sound so funny! 'Quarck, quarck, quarck, quarck, quarck, quarck, quarck!'

Every one stared in amazement. The spell must have gone wrong! Down the street hopped Tiddley-Pom – and whom should he meet at the corner but his wife, coming back from her shopping! When she saw Tiddley-Pom hopping along, quacking for all he was worth, she nearly fell over !

'Tiddley-Pom! What is the meaning of this?' she cried.

'Quarck, quarck!' said Tiddley.

'Don't quarck, quarck at me!' said Mrs Tiddley-Pom angrily. 'What are you behaving in this foolish manner for?'

'Quarck, quarck, quarck, quarck, quarck!'

said Tiddley, and went on hopping. His wife took hold of him and shook him angrily.

'Quarck, quarck,' said Tiddley sadly, and then as his wife shook him again, something flew out from behind his ear and fell on the ground! It was his pencil! He had put it behind his ear for safety, you remember – and had forgotten all about it!

'Quarck, quarck!' cried Tiddley joyfully, and picked it up. Then every one rushed up and began to explain things to Mrs Tiddley-Pom. How surprised she was! She took hold of Tiddley-Pom by the collar and walked him home, though he still tried to hop and quacked loudly all the way.

'You'll just go to bed until you stop quacking!' she said to him. 'And I hope that after you will try to remember where you put things! Hopping and quacking indeed, trying to find your pencil, and it's behind your ear all the time. You're a donkey, Tiddley-Pom, and you should bray, not quack!'

Well, Tiddley got better after a few days – but if he loses anything now, he gets very flustered, and begins to quack! It's funny to hear him.

'Quarck, quarck, quarck!' he says – and you may be sure Mrs Tiddley-Pom comes rushing out to see what he has lost.

THE CLEVER WHITE
KITTEN

Elsie was soon to have a birthday, and she felt most excited about it. She wondered if anyone would give her a pet for her birthday. She was very fond of animals and wanted one for her very own.

'If I had a puppy or a little kitten, how lovely it would be!' she said to herself. 'Or even a canary – but that would mean buying a cage, too, and that would be a lot of money. I should have to get a big cage too, because I wouldn't like to keep a canary in a tiny cage. Oh, dear, if only someone would buy me a pet!'

Elsie's mother had been thinking what to buy for Elsie, and she made up her mind to get her a nice workbasket, with a pair of scissors, a thimble, and reels of cotton in it. She thought Elsie would be so pleased to have one.

'What shall *I* buy for Elsie?' said the little

girl's daddy. 'I wonder if she'd like a pet?'

'Oh, I don't think so,' said Elsie's mother. 'She has never said she wanted a pet.'

That was quite true. Elsie had never said how much she would love an animal of her own. She had just hoped someone would buy her one. But they never seemed to think of a present like that!

Elsie's daddy couldn't think of anything else to buy her, so he thought he would just give her ten pounds to spend on herself. Elsie's mummy took the little girl with her to choose a nice workbasket at the shop, the day before her birthday.

The shop sold all sorts of baskets and leather goods. Elsie looked round. There were dog baskets and cat baskets, workbaskets, and shopping baskets, purses and suitcases, dog leads and collars. It was quite an exciting shop.

'I want a nice big workbasket for my little girl's birthday,' said Elsie's mother. The shop woman took some down. They were lovely, especially one, which was large and round, fitted inside with green silk on which lay a pair of shining scissors, a silver thimble, and four reels of cotton. Elsie liked it very much.

'I'll have that one,' said her mother. 'Will you send it round tonight, please? Thank you. And now I want to see purses for myself. Elsie, you can have a look round the shop whilst I choose them.'

So Elsie wandered round the shop, looking at everything – and then she suddenly saw the little white kitten!

It was lying fast asleep in a round dog basket, which was much too large for it! Elsie stroked it gently and it woke up at once. It stretched itself and yawned, and then rubbed its beautiful white head against the little girl's hand, purring loudly.

'Oh, you lovely, soft little thing!' said Elsie, cuddling the kitten against her. 'I wish you were mine! What fun we would have together! I would give you a little basket of your own, and you should have bread and milk for your breakfast every morning. I would buy you a blue ribbon for your soft, white neck, and we would have the loveliest games!'

The kitten purred more loudly than ever. It liked Elsie very much. It cuddled down against her and patted her with one little white paw.

Another shop girl came up and spoke to Elsie.

'The kitten is for sale,' she said. 'Would you like to buy it?'

'How much is it?' asked Elsie, remembering that she had one pound in her moneybox.

'Ten pounds,' said the shop girl. 'It is a very good kitten. Mrs Brown, the shopkeeper always gets ten pounds for the white kittens her cat has.'

'I've only got one pound,' said Elsie sadly. 'Oh, I wish Mummy had bought this kitten instead of the workbox.'

She ran up to her mother and pulled her arm. 'Mummy,' she said, 'I suppose I couldn't have something else instead of the workbasket, could I? I've just seen something much nicer.'

'No, Elsie,' said her mother. 'You can't change your mind like that. You know you want a workbasket, don't you?'

'Yes, I do,' said Elsie, 'but Mummy, this is a dear little . . .'

'It doesn't matter *what* it is,' said her mother, impatiently. 'You have chosen your basket, and I am sure you will like it better than anything else. Besides, the shop woman has made out the bill, and I have paid it. It is too late to change your mind now.'

Elsie was sorry. She had so badly wanted that kitten. Her eyes filled with tears, and she ran back to the corner where the little kitten was jumping up at a fly.

It leapt into her arms as she came near it, quite certain that this nice little girl was going to buy it and take it home. It wanted to live with Elsie. It was quite sure it would be happy with the kind little girl.

But Elsie stroked it and said no, she couldn't have it. 'I'm having a workbasket instead,' she told the kitten. 'That big round one there, on the counter. It is being sent round to my home tonight, so that I shall have it for my birthday in the morning. But, oh, kitten, I would so much rather have *you*!'

The kitten mewed and licked the back of Elsie's hand. It really was the dearest little kitten! It listened to all that Elsie said, and seemed to understand it.

'Goodbye,' said Elsie, seeing her mother beckoning to her. 'I wish you were mine!'

She went out of the shop with her mother, and the kitten was left alone, licking its fine white fur. It was thinking hard, for it was a very clever little kitten, especially when it wanted its own way. How could it go to that nice little girl? It wanted to live with her.

Then an idea came into its clever little mind.

It would creep into the big round basket that was to be sent to Elsie that night, and then it would go to the little girl – and when she opened the basket in the morning she would see the little white kitten there!

'She is sure to keep me if I go to her,' thought the kitten. It waited until the shop woman had gone to her tea that afternoon, and then it ran to the workbasket which stood ready to be packed up. The kitten quickly had lifted off the lid and had crept inside. There was just room for it to lie down. The lid

dropped down on top of it – and there it was, curled up inside the basket.

It didn't make a sound. It soon fell fast asleep, and didn't even wake up when the shop woman came to wrap the basket up in brown paper, ready for it to be taken to Elsie's home.

'Dear me! I didn't know this basket was so

heavy!' said the shop woman in surprise, but she didn't think of lifting up the lid to look inside! She gave the parcel to the shop girl to take to Elsie's house, and the girl carried it safely there, and gave it to Elsie's mother who opened the door.

That night Elsie's mother unwrapped the basket and set it on Elsie's chair, ready for the little girl to find when she came downstairs on her birthday morning. Her daddy put a little envelope on top of it with some money in. That was *his* birthday present to her. Next to the basket was a doll from her aunt, and a book from her granny. There was a pincushion from the cook, and a bottle of sweets from Jane the housemaid. So you see there were quite a lot of things waiting for Elsie!

Inside the workbasket was the kitten, too, waiting for Elsie. But nobody knew about that! When everyone had gone to sleep that night the kitten awoke. It lifted up the basket lid and crept out on to the chair. It wandered all round the house by itself, and smelt lots of mice.

'Ho!' said the kitten to itself. 'Mice! I shall have a fine time here! I shall catch all the mice there are!'

Soon the kitten crept back into the basket again and fell asleep until morning. First Daddy came in and took up the paper. The kitten hardly breathed! Then Mummy came in and arranged the breakfast things. The kitten nearly burst with excitement, for it knew that Elsie would soon be there!

Then there was the sound of someone singing happily, and into the room came Elsie, singing: 'It's my birthday, my birthday, my birthday!'

'Many happy returns of the day, little birthday girl!' cried Daddy and Mummy together, and they kissed her. 'Come and look at all your lovely presents.'

Elsie ran to her chair and looked at her presents. How pleased she was with them! The doll was lovely, the book was fine, the sweets were just what she wanted, the pincushion was just right for her dressing table, and there was a ten pound note from Daddy.

'And thank you, Mummy darling, for the lovely, lovely workbasket!' she cried – and she

opened the lid! There, curled up inside was the little white kitten, purring loudly its eyes blinking up at Elsie.

'Ooooooh!' screamed the little girl in the greatest surprise and delight. 'Ooh! Mummy! You darling, Mummy! What a surprise! Oh, you couldn't have given me anything I liked better! Oh, Mummy, I *shall* love this dear, little white kitten!'

She lifted it out of the basket and hugged it. Mummy and Daddy stared in the greatest astonishment. They knew nothing about the kitten at all. How had it got there?

'A kitten!' cried Mummy. 'Why, how did it get into the basket, Elsie? Where did it come from? I don't know anything about it.'

'But, Mummy, it's the one from the basket shop,' said Elsie. 'Didn't you buy it for me and put it in here for a lovely birthday surprise?'

'No, I didn't, dear,' said Mummy. 'You will have to take it back to the shop, I'm afraid. They will wonder what has become of it.'

'Then it isn't mine, after all?' asked Elsie, terribly disappointed. 'Oh, Mummy, I did so think it was for me. Oh, Mummy, I do want it.'

'But, darling, you can't possibly have it,' said Mummy. 'It isn't ours.'

Elsie sat down to breakfast, but her birthday was spoilt. She did so want the kitten. Now she had got to take it back to the shop. The kitten must have wanted to belong to her, or it would never have hidden itself in the basket. What a horrid disappointment.

Tears fell into her cornflakes and tears fell into her milk. Mummy saw them and was sorry.

'Don't cry, dear,' she said. 'It's your birthday, you know, and nobody must cry on birthdays. The postman hasn't been yet, and he may bring you some more parcels, so cheer up.'

But even when the postman brought five birthday cards and three more parcels for Elsie, she didn't cheer up. She wanted that kitten. She gave it some milk and it drank it all up. Then it flew round the room like a mad thing after a bumblebee. Then it curled up on Elsie's lap and fell asleep.

'You had better get your coat on, and Daddy and I will go with you to take the kitten back to the shop,' said Mummy. So Elsie sadly put on her coat, and Mummy put the kitten gently into a box with holes in it. Then Daddy carried it carefully, and Mummy took Elsie's hand, and they all set off to the shop.

Mummy was sorry when she saw Elsie's sad face. 'You are a silly child,' she said. 'Why didn't you tell me that you wanted a kitten for your birthday? Daddy would have given you one, or a puppy, if you really wanted one.'

'But Mummy, I did ask you yesterday if I could change the workbasket for the kitten,' said Elsie. 'But you said it was too late to change my mind.'

'Well, darling, I don't expect the shop would have let you have their kitten,' said Mummy. 'I'm sure the shop woman must be very fond of it, and wouldn't want to part with it.'

'But you don't *understand*, Mummy!' cried Elsie. 'The kitten was for sale, just like all the baskets and things. The shop girl said Mrs Brown always sold the white kittens, and she gets ten pounds for them. She said I could have this one if I liked, but you wouldn't let me change the basket.'

'Oh, darling, I didn't know you wanted a kitten so much!' said Mummy. 'What a pity!

I'm afraid we can't change the basket now.'

'Well, Elsie, you are a goose,' said Daddy suddenly. 'You really are a *goose*. What about *my* birthday present to you? Have you forgotten it?'

'No, Daddy,' said Elsie surprised. 'It was ten pounds to spend on myself.'

'And how much did you say this kitten was?' asked Daddy.

'Ten pounds,' said Elsie, and she suddenly stopped in the middle of the pavement and clapped her hands for joy. 'Oh, Daddy! Ten pounds! I could *buy* the kitten myself with your present to me. Can I?'

'Of course,' said Daddy. 'Can't she, Mummy?'

'Yes,' said Mummy, pleased. 'So, Elsie, instead of taking the kitten back to leave it at the shop, we'll go and *buy* it!'

You should have seen Elsie's face! It was shining all over with joy! She had Daddy's ten pounds safely in her purse, so she could buy the kitten at once.

The shop woman *was* surprised when she heard what Daddy had to say about the kitten.

'Hidden inside the workbasket!' she cried. 'Well, what a very strange thing! I hunted all over the place last night for the little thing, and I couldn't find it anywhere. It must have wanted to go and live with Elsie.'

'It *does* want to,' said Elsie eagerly. 'So may I buy it? It's my birthday today and Daddy has given me ten pounds. Here it is. May I take the kitten home again now?'

'Certainly,' said the shop woman, smiling. 'But wait a minute – if it's your birthday I'd like to give you a little present, too. Look, here is a nice little round basket for your kitten to sleep in. It's the one she has been used to, so she will love it.'

'Oh, thank you!' cried Elsie in delight. 'This is the very nicest birthday I've ever had! I shall *love* that little white kitten. I shall call it Snowball, and play with it all the day long!'

So she does – and you should see Snowball now! She is the fattest, prettiest, naughtiest kitten you ever saw, but everyone loves her. Mummy often tells people how Snowball hid herself in Elsie's workbasket because she wanted to live with Elsie, and the listening kitten pricks up its ears and says: 'Miaow! Miaow!' Which means, 'Quite right! I meant to get what I wanted, and I got it!'

THE DOLL ON THE CHRISTMAS TREE

Raggy was a funny little doll. She was called Raggy because she was stuffed with rags, and was very soft and cuddly. But she was old now, and her face looked funny. She had odd eyes, her hair was made of yellow wool, her nose was flat, and her teeth and lips were made of white and red stitches.

Every Christmas the children sorted out their old toys, and put aside those that they could spare. They were given away to children who had very few toys. But Raggy was never given away because the children loved her so much.

That Christmas a great many new toys came to the nursery. There were three children there, and they all had aunts and uncles who gave them lovely toys. So a new railway train came, a new clockwork motorcar, three new dolls, a doll's house, a beautiful panda and a blue teddy bear.

The old toys looked at the new ones, and thought how clean and shining and beautiful they were. The new toys looked at the old ones, and turned up their noses at them.

'What a dirty creature you are!' said the new blue bear to the old brown one.

'What a battered creature you are!' said the new panda to the old one.

Then all the new toys stared at Raggy.

'Are you a doll or a bit of rubbish?' asked the new curly-haired doll.

'Why don't you wash your dirty old clothes?' asked the doll with the red hair ribbon.

'I hope we haven't got to live in the same toy cupboard as *you*,' said the new sailor doll. 'You smell horrid – old and dirty!'

Raggy felt sad. She *was* old and she *was* dirty. She couldn't wash her clothes because they

were sewn on to her, and she couldn't get them off. She sometimes tried to brush her yellow hair, but it is difficult to brush wool and make it look neat. Usually brushing her woollen hair made it very fuzzy indeed.

'I'm sorry I look so old and dirty,' said Raggy. 'I hope you will be happy in this nursery. The three children are very kind.'

'We should be happy if we didn't have to live with people like you, and the dirty old teddy and the battered old panda,' said the curly-haired doll unkindly.

'Now stop talking like that,' said big Jumbo from his corner. 'We have lived here for years, and the nursery is ours. You are newcomers. Behave yourselves.'

'The idea! Talking to us like that!' said the blue bear. 'I've a good mind to take that elephant by his tail and pull him out of the nursery! He should live in the boxroom, not here. He's quite out of date!'

Jumbo was so angry that he ran at the bear and nearly knocked him over. The bear skipped neatly out of the way. 'That elephant has no manners at all!' growled the bear. 'What sort of a nursery is this that we've come into?'

Now the three children were giving a party after Christmas to all their friends. They wrote out the invitations and posted them. They dressed the big Christmas tree in the hall, and covered it with shining ornaments and candles, and long gleaming strips of tin-foil that shone like icicles.

Then they tied little presents on the tree for their guests. It looked simply lovely.

But when they went to buy a fairy doll for

the tree, they couldn't get one anywhere!

'Sorry, but we have none this year,' all the shops said. The children were bitterly disappointed. They talked about it in the nursery, and all the toys listened.

'We *must* have a fairy doll at the top of the tree,' said Hilda. 'It doesn't look right unless we do.'

'A fairy doll is magic, and she can do magic with her wand,' said Ken. 'Everyone knows that.'

'I wonder if we'd better put one of our new toys at the top of the tree instead?' said Polly.

All the new toys picked up their ears at that.

My goodness — to be at the top of the Christmas tree would be a very fine thing!

'I should look sweet there,' said the curly-haired doll.

'I am just about the right size,' said the doll with the red hair ribbon.

'A sailor doll at the top of the tree would be marvellous,' said the sailor doll.

'I'm sure all the children would rather have *me* than you,' said the panda, proudly.

'They would shout with delight if *I* was there!' said the blue bear.

Raggy listened to them all and sighed. It would be marvellous to be at the top of the Christmas tree, watching the lighted candles shine, and the ornaments glitter. 'But I must be glad that I wasn't put in the dustbin this year,' thought the little raggy doll. 'After all, I *am* very old and very dirty!'

Now the children's mother was sorry because her three children were so disappointed about the fairy doll. She wondered what she could do about it. One night, when they were in bed, she went into the nursery and looked into the toy cupboard. All the new toys were thrilled. They felt sure she had come to choose one of them to put at the top of the tree.

So she had — but she didn't somehow think that any of the toys in the cupboard were quite right for the tree.

Raggy wasn't in the cupboard. The curly-haired doll had turned her out that night. 'We are not going to let you share the cupboard with us,' she said. 'You are so ugly and old and dirty. You ought to be in the dustbin.'

Raggy had gone to a corner and curled up there, very miserable. It was bad enough to be old and dirty, without being told so a dozen times a day.

Mother shut the cupboard door, and then she suddenly saw Raggy curled up in the corner. She picked her up and looked at her.

'Dear little doll!' she said. 'Hilda had you when she was a baby, and all the children have loved you, little Raggy.'

She carried Raggy out of the nursery with her. She went to her workroom, and there she set to work on the old doll. She unpicked her dirty clothes, and there lay Raggy on the table without any clothes at all, feeling rather cold and strange.

'You are going to be a beautiful doll, old Raggy!' said Mother. 'I am going to make you a dress of finest gauze, with frilly skirts, and little silver beads all over it! I shall make you shining silver wings, and give you a beautiful wand to wave. I shall wash your yellow woollen hair and make it shine like gold. I shall give you a silver crown to wear! How pleased the children will be!'

Mother worked hard all the evening. She made Raggy a lovely frilly dress sewn with tiny silver beads. She made her a most beautiful pair of silver wings that stuck out behind Raggy like real ones. She washed Raggy's woollen hair and dried it, and it looked clean and golden. She made a silver crown and a silver wand, and she even made a little pair of silver shoes!

'There! You look lovely!' said Mother. 'The prettiest fairy doll we have ever had, Raggy! I'll put you at the top of the tree!'

The next morning the children shouted in delight to see a fairy doll on the tree. 'Mother! You got one after all! Oh, Mother, she's beautiful!'

Many children came to the party. They stared at the lovely fairy doll, and how they all longed

to have her for their own! They talked about her as they sat at tea in the nursery.

'She's simply wonderful,' they said. 'She ought to be queen of the nursery, Hilda. She's the finest fairy doll we've ever seen. And she has such a sweet look on her face too – so kind and loving!'

The toys listened to all this. That night, when the children had gone, they talked together. 'Let us go and see this beautiful fairy doll. Perhaps she would come and live here with us and be our queen. We haven't a queen. It would be a great thing if we could have a fairy doll for a queen, because then she could use the magic in her wand for us!'

So they all crept down into the hall to see the tree. The candles were no longer lit. The tree stood there in the moonlight, its ornaments shining and its fairy doll looking mysterious and beautiful at the top.

'Look at her wings!' whispered the blue bear.

'Look at her wand!' said the curly-haired doll.

'It's a pity that ugly old Raggy isn't here to see her,' said Jumbo. 'I can't think where she has disappeared to. I hope she hasn't been put into the dustbin.'

'Best place for her!' said the sailor doll. 'My goodness me – how I love that fairy doll! I wish she would marry me and work some magic for me!'

Jumbo spoke humbly to the fairy doll. 'Beautiful fairy doll, will you come and be our queen? We would be very proud of you.'

'Thank you,' said the fairy doll, in a voice that sounded rather familiar. 'But are you quite sure you want me?'

'Of course!' said everyone. 'Come down now and we will give a party for you, fairy doll!'

So the fairy doll climbed down from the tree and went with the toys to the nursery. Raggy didn't know that the toys thought she was a really-truly fairy doll. She thought they knew she was only Raggy dressed up. She smiled round at everyone, as happy as could be, and the toys loved her.

What a fuss they made of her! They told her dozens of times how beautiful she was. Raggy had never had such a wonderful time in her life!

And then the curly-haired doll said: 'It's a pity that dirty old Raggy isn't here, fairy doll! Perhaps you could have waved your wand over her and made her a bit cleaner and prettier. She *was* such an ugly creature!'

The fairy doll looked at the curly-haired doll, and then she spoke in her soft little voice.

'Don't you know that *I* am Raggy? It is true that I am a fairy doll now, too – but I am

Raggy as well!'

All the toys stared in the greatest amazement – and then they saw that it was indeed Raggy – but what a different Raggy!

'Oh, Raggy – you haven't been put in the dustbin after all!' cried Jumbo, joyfully. 'Dear little Raggy – you deserve to be queen, you deserve to be a fairy doll, because you have always been so good and kind. Your Majesty, I am delighted to see you again!'

All the old toys crowded round Raggy and fussed her. The new ones felt most awkward – dear me, suppose Raggy had magic in her wand and could punish them for their unkindness now! They thought they had better be nice to her too.

But Raggy knew what they were thinking. 'I

78

won't be your queen if you don't want me to be,' she said. 'I'll just be queen of the old toys. And don't think that I shall use the magic in my wand to punish you. I shall only use it to make you happy.'

'Oh,' said the curly-haired doll, staring at Raggy in surprise. 'Oh! You *are* kind and good and forgiving. You deserve to be queen, you really do!'

'She does,' said the sailor doll.

'She's a darling!' said the blue bear. And all the new toys curtsied and bowed to Raggy most politely and gracefully.

She is still queen of the nursery, and each Christmas she goes back to the top of the Christmas tree. I expect you'd like to see her there, wouldn't you? Well, if you get to know

Hilda, Ken and Polly, just ask them to show you old Raggy. They will be delighted to!

WHAT HAPPENED
TO EPPIE?

Eppie was a little shepherd boy. He looked after sheep on the mountain side, and his uncle watched them with him. They had two dogs, swift runners, who could outrun any wolf and hunt it down.

There were many, many sheep, spread all over the mountain side. Sometimes Eppie had to go up and down, seeking for two or three that had strayed, or had hurt themselves. A dog went with him then for company. Eppie liked the spring and the summer, for then the days were golden and the nights were warm. But when the winter came he shivered and wished that he could be a little town boy, safe in a warm house at night, instead of taking turns with his uncle at watching the sheep.

The big, grey wolves were hungry in the wintertime, and came slinking out of their mountain lairs to hunt for food. Sometimes they came to the flock of sheep and stole a lamb. Eppie had to watch for the creeping form against the side of the hill, outlined by the moonlight. Then he would give the alarm, and the dogs would wake and race after the wolf.

One winter Eppie was lazy and discontented. He grumbled all day long and his uncle grew vexed with him.

'You are a young lad, and must learn to work,' said his uncle sharply. 'Enough of this grumbling, Eppie!'

'This is no life for a boy,' sulked Eppie. 'I hate the silly grey sheep. I hate the stupid, skipping lambs.'

'You are a bad boy to say such things,' said his uncle. 'The sheep give us warm clothes and good meat, and as for the little lambs, they are pretty creatures and sweet to watch in the springtime. You cannot help loving such inno-cent things. Let me hear no more of your stu-pidity, Eppie.'

Eppie said no more, for he was afraid of his tall, strong uncle, with his brown weather-beaten face. The shepherd was a fine man, tender with the little lambs and good to the sheep when they were hurt or needed his help. He could not understand why Eppie did not love the flock as he did.

That night Eppie had to watch the sheep. It was cold, and the moon shone pale in the sky. Eppie shivered and pulled his rug round him. The two dogs lay at his feet, tired out with a long run that afternoon, rounding up stray sheep. They lay with their noses to their feet, dreaming of rabbits and wolves.

Eppie's uncle was in a hut a good way up the mountain. Round it were sheltering hurdles to keep in the sheep that had little new-born lambs. The shepherd was going to be up all night, tending them, and he had warned Eppie to keep a good watch that night.

'The big grey wolf is about,' he said. 'He took a sheep from over the hills, so I heard, not three days ago. Watch well, Eppie.'

Eppie did not answer. He turned away, sulking. He was tired, and wanted to sleep. He felt sure that his uncle had made up the tale about the wolf, in order to frighten him and make him alert.

'There's no wolf about!' he thought. 'I don't believe my uncle's tale.'

He sat in the shelter of a rock, wrapped in a thick blanket. The stars were pale in the moonlight. He could see clearly the valley, below, with black shadows here and there, cast by bushes and trees. Nothing moved but the grey sheep, and even they were very still that night.

There were some tiny lambs here and there with their mothers, and they lifted their heads, maa-ing now and again.

Eppie felt sleepy. He knew he should get up and walk about to keep himself awake. But he was sulky and bad tempered, and would not move. His eyes kept shutting.

'What does it matter if I sleep?' he thought. 'No wolf will come! And if one does come, what will happen? A few lambs will be frightened, and maybe one carried off. Shepherds expect that now and again. What do I care for the silly lambs? I shall sleep!'

He closed his eyes, and soon, like the two dogs, he was fast asleep and dreaming. Two hours passed. No wolf came – but someone else did! The boy's uncle stole down the hill like a black shadow, come to tell Eppie to go to the hut and take his rest whilst he watched instead. When he found Eppie fast asleep he was very angry. He saw the boy's sulky face, and then was sad, too. Eppie had to be a shepherd, and until he cared for the flock, and loved the lambs, he would not be happy. The shepherd looked down at the sleeping boy, and then sat quietly down by him. He began to murmur a tale into the boy's ear – and Eppie dreamed the tale!

In his dream he was a lamb, small and long-legged, with a wriggling tail. He was on the mountain side in the warm sunshine, skipping all about with joy. His small brother was with him, and together they bounded here and there, rushing to their big warm mother when she baa-ed at them. Life was good. Everything was warm, and the little lamb was full of delight.

But when the night came it was different. The big golden ball in the sky went away, and

the darkness came. The moon rose, but it was not full and gave only a pale light to the world. Everything looked different. The air was cold and the tiny lamb shivered. He cuddled close to his mother and she licked him and his little brother tenderly.

The lamb had heard of the wolf, but it was only at night that he was afraid of it.

'What is the wolf?' he asked his mother.

'It is a great grey shape in the night-time,' answered his mother. 'It has red, gleaming eyes and fearful gleaming teeth. It comes like a shadow, and eats little lambs like you. So keep close to me.'

The lamb cuddled even closer, and maa-ed in fright.

'Do not be afraid,' said the mother sheep, comfortingly. 'We have a good shepherd to watch over us, and a boy, too. There are two dogs, besides. See, the boy is watching us now, through the night, and if the wolf should come, he will give the alarm and wake the dogs. Then they will chase the wolf away and no harm will be done!'

After that the mother sheep fell asleep, and the lamb and his brother closed his eyes and slept, too – but in a short while the little lamb awakened with a start, full of fear. He stared round in the night. The moon was behind a cloud and the mountain side was in darkness. What had wakened him?

A feeling of dreadful fear came over the little creature. Something terrible was near him. What was it? And then he saw two red, gleaming eyes in the darkness! It was the wolf, the wolf! It was looking at him. It was coming to take him away!

Where was the shepherd boy? Could he not see the wolf? Would he not send the dogs chasing after him down the hill side? Oh, shepherd boy, wake up, wake up! The two eyes came nearer still, and the little lamb dared not move. He could hear the wolf sniffing, and then he felt the animal's hot breath over him.

'Maa-aa!' he called, pressing against his mother. She woke and smelt the wolf at once. In terror she scrambled to her feet and bounded away, calling loudly to her two lambs. One ran with her – but the other, who had waked to see the wolf near, could not get away. The wolf bared his teeth and snatched at him.

'Maa-aa!' bleated the lamb piteously. Where, oh where was the shepherd boy? Surely he could not be asleep? Where were the two swift running dogs?

The wolf picked up the shivering lamb in his sharp teeth and made off with him. 'Maa-aa,

maa-aa!' bleated the lamb in terror. Then the whole flock was aroused and bunched together quickly, baa-ing loudly. The two dogs awoke, rushed here and there, trying to get the trail of the wolf. They quickly found it and were after him in a trice.

The little lamb heard the dogs barking. The wolf gripped him even more tightly in his teeth and the lamb bleated in pain. Suddenly the two dogs appeared, one on each side of the wolf, and the wolf dropped the lamb, bared its teeth and faced the dogs. The lamb lay still, terrified. He was not badly hurt, but so full of fear that he could not even move his head.

The dogs leaped on the wolf, and it backed away snarling. The lamb heard the fighting getting farther and farther away, and then suddenly saw a swinging light. Was it another wolf? He maa-ed in terror – but it was the lantern of the shepherd. Then the tiny lamb felt himself gathered up in the arms of someone who loved him and he was full of peace and happiness. He was safe.

The little shepherd boy, whose dream this was, suddenly felt himself picked up in someone's strong arms. He was the little lamb and the shepherd boy, too. How strange! He awoke and opened his eyes. Now he was only a shepherd boy, out on the mountain side. He was no longer a wolf-hunted lamb. He was in the arms of his uncle, the shepherd who was carrying him up the mountain side to the hut.

'Uncle, Uncle, put me down; there is a wolf among the sheep!' he cried, struggling, half

remembering his strange dream. 'Oh, quick, the little lambs will be so frightened. They may be caught in the teeth of that big grey wolf. Oh, uncle, let me go and see if the sheep are all right. Let me take the dogs!'

'There is no wolf tonight,' said his uncle. 'You are tired with your long day with the dogs, Eppie. I came to take your place, and found you sleeping, so I am carrying you to the hut. It seemed a shame to wake you.'

'Uncle, I had such a strange dream,' said Eppie, remembering how he had seemed to be a little lamb. 'Do you know how frightened a lamb can be, Uncle? I dreamed I was caught by a wolf. It was terrible. I shall never sleep again when it is my turn to watch! The sheep trust us, Uncle, don't they?'

'Yes,' said his uncle. 'I think you will be a good shepherd boy now, won't you, Eppie?'

'Yes, always,' said Eppie, and he meant it. 'It is a grand thing to be a shepherd, Uncle. One day I shall be the best shepherd in the kingdom, and have the biggest flocks in the world!'

THE FOUR-LEAVED CLOVER

'Linda!' called Mother. 'It's time to go to your dancing lesson. Hurry up!'

Mother didn't need to tell Linda to hurry for her dancing lesson! It was the lesson Linda liked best of all, and she didn't mind a bit giving up Saturday morning for it. She was always ready at least ten minutes before the bus went.

She came running downstairs, wearing her little, white fluffy dress, with her coat over it. She had her dancing shoes in her bag.

'Here's the money for the bus,' said Mother, and gave it to her. 'Got your shoes – and a clean hanky?'

'Yes, of course!' said Linda. 'I'll go now, Mother. Hurray, it's dancing lesson today!'

Linda was a very good dancer, very quick at learning all kinds of new steps.

'You're as light as a fairy!' the dancing teacher said to her that morning. 'I really feel sometimes that you must have wings, Linda, wings we can't see, the way you leap here and there, and come down without the slightest sound!'

Linda wished she *was* a fairy! How marvellous to have wings and to be able to fly! But she had never seven seen a fairy, though she had hidden behind trees for hours and watched.

'Mother,' she said one day, 'is there any way that people can have wishes come true nowadays?'

'Well,' said Mother, 'there aren't any fairies about here to give you a wish – and there are no wishing-wands for sale, and certainly no wishing-caps. You'll just have to find a four-leaved clover!'

'A four-leaved clover!' said Linda. 'But a clover has three leaves, not four.'

'I know,' said Mother, 'but sometimes, just *sometimes*, you can find one with four leaves on the stem, instead of three. And that's supposed to have a little magic in it.'

'*Really?*' said Linda, excited. 'What kind of magic?'

'Well – a four-leaved clover is always lucky,' said Mother, 'and some of them are supposed to be magic enough to grant one wish – but only one. I've never found one – they're very rare.'

'I shall go and look in the clover patches on the lawn till I *do* find one!' said Linda. 'And I know what I shall wish when I do! I shall wish I was a fairy with wings, and could fly!'

'Oh dear,' said Mother. 'Don't wish that – I'd rather have you as you are, a little girl!'

'I suppose I couldn't be both,' said Linda. 'What a pity. But if I *do* find a four-leaved clover, I shall simply *have* to wish I could be a fairy with wings and fly, Mother. You don't know how badly I want to.'

Now, will you believe it, the third time that Linda went to hunt for a four-leaved clover on the lawn, she found one! At first she couldn't believe her eyes – but there it was! She picked it very carefully indeed.

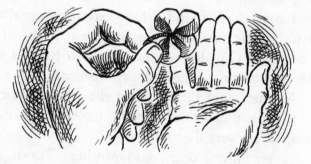

'You've got four leaves, not three,' she said, and her voice shook with excitement. 'You're magic! I'm going to wish my wish. Are you listening clover?'

The clover shook in the breeze. Linda held it up and wished. 'I wish I could be a fairy with wings, and fly in the air!'

She waited. Would she turn into a fairy straightaway, with wings on her back? Did they take time to grow? She wondered if she would feel them growing. How soon would she be able to fly?

Nothing happened. She put her hand round to her back to see if any wings were sprouting. If they were she would have to go indoors and ask Mother to cut holes in her clothes so that they could grow out.

But nothing was growing there. She couldn't even feel any little bumps which would tell her that wings were coming. It was really very disappointing.

'I must have found a four-leaved clover that isn't magic enough to grant me a wish,' she thought. 'Oh, dear – and I was so pleased to think I might really have my wish at last!'

'Mother,' said Linda, when she went indoors, 'I found a four-leaved clover – look! But it isn't magic. It's very disappointing.'

'Never mind, dear,' said Mother. 'Put it in between the pages of your favourite book. It will always be lucky, even if it doesn't grant a wish!'

It was Saturday afternoon, and Linda had

already had her dancing lesson that morning. It was three o'clock now – what should she do till tea time?

'Mother, I'll take Scamper for a walk,' she said. 'He's longing to go!'

So she set off with Scamper. She walked down the lane and came to the main road. She thought she would go into the town and look at the toy shops.

As she passed the Town Hall, she stopped to look at a big poster there.

'GRAND SHOW TONIGHT,' said the poster. 'PANTOMIME FOR CHILDREN.'

'Oh, dear – I wish I'd known, then perhaps Mother would have taken me,' thought Linda. 'Now I expect all the tickets will be gone.'

She went to ask. Yes, every single one had been sold. What a pity!

As she stood looking at the pictures in the

porch of the Town Hall, two or three people came out from the hall itself.

'Well, the rehearsal went all right,' said one of them. 'But *what* are we going to do about that child who has been taken ill? Can we possibly replace her?'

'I shouldn't think so,' said another man. 'We *must* have someone who can dance. Pity – the show won't be quite so good with one dancer less.'

Someone else came out and joined them. It was Miss Clarissa, Linda's dancing teacher. She caught sight of the little girl and smiled. Then she suddenly stopped as if a thought had struck her. She went quickly up to the three men.

'I've got an idea. Do you see that little girl over there? Well, I teach her dancing, and she's as light as a fairy! I believe she could easily take the place of the child who is ill!'

The three men looked at Linda, and she went very red. 'Would you like to be one of the fairies in the pantomime tonight?' asked Miss Clarissa. 'You know all the steps of the dance, and if any are different you can easily follow the dancers in front of you.'

'But – but – what would my mother say?' said Linda, amazed.

'Go and ask her,' said one of the men. 'Go along and ask her now! Take her home, Miss

Clarissa. If you think she's good enough, we'll have her. The dress will fit all right.'

'Come along, Linda,' said Miss Clarissa, and hurried her off. She talked to her as they went along. 'There's a most beautiful dress to wear, and you have a wand and a pair of wings! You'll be just like a fairy!'

Linda could hardly speak. 'Will I fly?' she said at last.

'Well, we shall put you on a wire, with the other fairies,' said Miss Clarissa, 'and swing you to and fro across the stage, and up and down – and you must flap your lovely wings, of course!'

'Oh,' said Linda, and her eyes shone. 'My wish is coming true!' she thought. 'It is, it is! I wished to be a fairy, and have wings, and fly – and it's all going to happen! Mother said she still wanted me to be her own little girl, even if I was a fairy – and I shall be! I shall be a fairy and fly just for tonight!'

Well, Mother was just as excited as Linda, of course. She nodded her head to all that Miss Clarissa said.

'I know it will please Linda,' she said. 'She will feel like a real fairy, flying through the air like that. Why, Linda, your four-leaved clover was magic, after all!'

That night Linda went to the pantomime,

but she didn't sit in the seats in front to watch. She was behind with all the rest of the cast. There were about twenty small girls who were to dance – but only four of them were to fly – and one of those four was Linda!

The fairy costume fitted her beautifully, and she trembled with joy when she put on her beautiful, big silvery wings. 'Move your shoulders to and fro, and the wings will flap,' said Miss Clarissa. Linda moved her shoulders – and sure enough the wings flapped as if they were really growing out of her back.

'Here is your wand,' said Miss Clarissa.

Linda took it. 'Is there any magic in it?' she asked.

'No,' said Miss Clarissa. 'Not as much as in your four-leaved clover, anyway! I never heard of a little girl before who wished to be a fairy with wings, and fly – and whose wish came true in such a wonderful way. Now let me just see you do your steps. Linda – I'm sure you will dance as lightly as anyone.'

'Is my mother watching – and Daddy?' asked Linda. 'Have they got seats?'

'Yes, right in the very front,' said Miss Clarissa. 'You won't be frightened when you fly in the air, will you, Linda?'

'Of course not,' said Linda. 'It's what I'm looking forward to most of all!'

The time came for the fairies to go on stage. They skipped on, waving their wands, and began to dance. Linda danced best of all. She couldn't help it, she was so happy. She really was as light as a fairy, and soon everyone was

watching the little girl with dark hair and dark eyes, dancing as if she was in a lovely dream.

Then came the part where four of the fairies were to fly! Linda and the other three had strong wires fixed to them, and, quite suddenly, they were lifted right off their feet into the air! Linda wasn't expecting it, and she gasped for joy. Her wings flapped gently, and she laughed in delight.

'I'm flying,' she thought. 'I'm flying! So this is what flying is like – lovelier even than I thought! Oh, I'm glad my wish came true!'

The fairies were clapped and clapped. Then somebody called out: 'Where's the little dark

fairy? She was the best of all – she's a *real* fairy!'

Miss Clarissa pushed Linda out on to the stage alone. She was bewildered. She didn't curtsey, because she didn't know why she had been pushed alone on to the stage. Then suddenly the wire pulled her up into the air once more, and she gave a scream of delight.

'I'm flying again!' she cried. 'I'm flying!'

Everyone laughed and clapped madly. Her mother almost cried with pride and delight as she watched Linda flying gracefully to and fro all by herself. Then the wire swung her down to the stage again, and she remembered to curtsey.

'Well done, Linda,' said Miss Clarissa, pleased, when Linda came running off, still flapping her wings. 'Come and see the stage manager – he's delighted.'

'Good girl!' said the big stage manager to Linda. 'Now, I want to give you a present for being such a good fairy. What would you like. Ask for any toy you want!'

Linda's eyes shone. 'I don't want a toy,' she said. 'But – oh – do you think I could *possibly* keep my fairy wings?'

'Of course,' said the man. 'I suppose you think you'll go flying off every night on them? Well, happy journeys!'

Linda couldn't get to sleep that night. Her wings were on a chair beside her bed. She put her hand out every now and again and touched

them to make sure they were still there.

'My wish came true!' she kept thinking. 'I didn't believe it would, but it did – in a really magic way! Oh! I'm glad I found that four-leaved clover. Perhaps one day I'll find another and wish that I can fly again.'

Perhaps she will. I hope *you* find a four-leaved clover, too. Take care of it if you do!

DAME QUICKLY'S WASHTUB

One day when Tickle the pixie was going home, he passed by Dame Quickly's cottage. He thought he would peep round and see what he could see. Dame Quickly often used magic spells, and it was fun to watch her.

But there was nobody in the cottage. On the table, by itself, stood something that made Tickle's eyes gleam. It was a washtub, a bright yellow one, as magic as could be.

Everyone knew Dame Quickly's washtub. You had only to put your dirty clothes in it, and say, 'Alla malla, washtub, get to work!' and the washtub would swish the clothes round and round, clean them beautifully, and then wring them out and throw them on to the table.

'I wish I could borrow that washtub,' thought Tickle, thinking of the big wash he had to do that afternoon. 'What a pity Dame Quickly is out. I suppose she has gone to her sister's for the day. She always does on Monday.'

He looked and looked at the washtub. Then he climbed in at the window and picked it up.

'It can't matter borrowing it,' he thought. 'I know I ought to ask – but if I wait till tomorrow and ask Dame Quickly, she might say no. So I'd better borrow it now. I can take it back before she comes home tonight. She won't even know I borrowed it!'

He ran off with it on his shoulders. When he got home he filled it with warm water, put some soap into the water, and then threw in all his dirty clothes and linen.

Then he tapped the tub three times and cried, 'Alla, malla, washtub, get to work!'

And my goodness me, you should have seen that washtub dealing with those clothes! It swished them round and round in the soapy water and got all the dirt out as quickly as could be.

Then it tossed them out on to the table, with all the water wrung out, ready for Tickle to rinse. It was marvellous.

Tickle took them to rinse in the sink. The washtub made a curious whistling noise, and suddenly the curtains flew from the window and put themselves into the water. Then the washtub set to work on them.

'Hi!' cried Tickle. 'Don't do that. Those curtains were only washed last week. Now I shall have to dry them and iron them all over again. Stop, you silly washtub.'

But the washtub took no notice. It tossed the washed curtains out of the water, and then whistled again.

And into the tub jumped all the rugs and mats off the floor! It was most annoying.

Tickle shouted crossly. 'Will you stop behaving like this? I don't want my mats washed. Stop it, you silly washtub.'

Out came the rugs and mats as clean as could be – and then the washtub whistled again. All the cushions threw themselves into the tub! But that was too much for Tickle.

'I won't have my nice feather cushions soaked with water! Now, stop it, washtub!'

The tub whistled again – and, oh dear, poor Tickle found himself jumping into the washtub

too! He was swished round and round, well-soaped, squeezed, and tossed out on to the table.

'You wicked washtub!' he cried, wiping the soap from his eyes. 'You wicked –'

The tub whistled, and into the water went Tickle again! This was a fine game, the washtub thought, a very fine game indeed. It waited till Tickle had been thrown out once more, then whistled again – and in went poor Tickle, splash!

When he was tossed out for the third time he

fled to the door. He ran down the road to meet Dame Quickly's bus. Oh, oh, oh, she must get her horrid washtub as soon as she could! Who would have thought it would behave like that?

Dame Quickly stepped off the bus. Tickle ran up to her, dripping with water.

'Dame Quickly, dear Dame Quickly, please, please come and get your washtub from my house!' begged Tickle. 'It is behaving so badly.'

'From your house?' said Dame Quickly, in surprise. 'How did my washtub get into your house?'

Tickle felt rather awkward. 'Well, you see,' he said, 'I – er – I wanted to borrow it – but you were out – so I er – I – er –'

'You took it without asking!' said Dame Quickly, looking very stern. 'Don't you know that's a very wrong thing to do? You knew I wouldn't lend it to you if you asked me – so you took it without asking. That's next door to stealing, you know that. You bad little pixie. Well – keep the washtub. I can make myself another.'

'Oh!' squealed poor Tickle, 'I can't keep it. I really can't. It keeps on whistling me into the water, and washing me. Oh, do, do come and get it.'

Dame Quickly laughed. 'What a strange, lovely punishment for you,' she said. 'No – I tell you I don't want my tub back.'

'But I shall spend the rest of my life being whistled into the water and washed!' wailed Tickle.

'That's quite likely,' said Dame Quickly. 'Goodbye.'

Tickle caught hold of her skirt, and wept big tears down his cheeks. 'Please, I'll never borrow without asking again, please, I'm sorry. What can I do to show you I am sorry?'

'Ah, now you are talking properly,' said Dame Quickly. 'If you are really sorry, and want to make up for what you have done, I'll come and get the tub. But for the next three weeks, I shall expect you to come and do my ironing for me.'

She went back to Tickle's cottage, spoke sharply to the tub, which had begun to whistle as soon as it saw Tickle again, and then put it on her shoulder.

'Now, remember,' she said to Tickle, 'come each Tuesday for three weeks to do my ironing. And maybe at the end of that time you will have made up your mind that it really isn't good to borrow without asking! Goodbye!'

Poor Tickle. He'll be very careful now, won't he?

ONE DARK NIGHT

Thomas was a funny boy. He was so scared of things! He couldn't bear to sing alone in class. He couldn't bear to take anyone's dog for a walk in case it ran away. He hated going upstairs by himself at night, and he always had to have a night-light in his room, because he was afraid of the dark.

'I just want to tell you this, Thomas,' said his father one day. 'I'm not going to force you to be brave – to jump into the sea, or to climb a tree, or anything like that. Nobody can make you brave except yourself. But listen – if ever you have to be brave for *somebody else's* sake, then that is the time you simply *must* have courage!'

'I see, Daddy,' said Thomas. 'You mean – even though I feel as if I can't jump into the swimming pool quickly, like all the others do – if I saw somebody fall into the river, for *their* sake I'd have to jump in straight away and rescue them.'

'That's just what I mean, Thomas,' said his father, pleased. 'Please remember that. It's very, very important. The *real* coward is always somebody who fails other people.'

Thomas did think about that, but nothing seemed to happen to other people to make him try and be brave! He was secretly very glad. He didn't even *want* to be brave.

Then one night he heard his little sister Janet crying in her bedroom. He called out to her. 'Janet – what's the matter?'

'Oh, Thomas – I've left my doll out in the garden,' said Janet. 'And I know it's going to rain. She'll get wet, and she'll get a cold, and she'll be so frightened and lonely out there.'

'She won't,' said Thomas.

'She will,' said Janet. 'I'm going out to get her. Poor Rosebud! She'll be so afraid of the dark.'

'You can't go out in the night all by yourself!' said Thomas, sitting up in bed. 'Don't be silly. You're too little.'

'I don't feel little,' said Janet. 'All the same . . .

I wish *you'd* go Thomas. You're much bigger than me.'

Thomas didn't want to go. The very idea of creeping down the dark garden at night made him shiver. Then he thought of what his father had said.

'The real coward is always someone who fails other people!'

'I ought to go instead of Janet,' he said to himself. 'She's afraid but she's going. I'm afraid, too – and as it's for Janet, I *must* go! Oh, dear!'

'Janet!' he called. 'Get back into bed. I'll go and get Rosebud. Where is she?'

'Down by the henhouse,' said Janet, getting thankfully back into bed. 'Oh, Thomas – you *are* brave!'

Thomas felt a little better. It was nice to be thought brave, even though he was hating every minute of this night walk! He slipped downstairs and out into the garden.

It was very dark indeed. He bumped into a bush. Something flew round his head – was it a bat? He switched on his torch, but no light came! The battery had gone. This was worse than ever!

He groped his way down the garden in the dark, his heart thumping. He was afraid something might grab him – though there was nothing to grab him at all! He was afraid of hurting himself, he was afraid all the time.

He came to the henhouse and wondered where Rosebud was. He saw a little white patch on the steps of the henhouse and felt for it. It was Rosebud – good!

He picked up the doll and was just going back to the house when he heard voices – low voices, nearby. He stood quite still, scared. Who was about at this time of night?

He stepped into the hedge close by, his heart thumping again. The voices were nearer now, and he could hear very quiet footsteps.

'No one about!' whispered someone. 'This is the place, isn't it? Let's hope the hens don't make too much noise! Got the sack!'

And then Thomas knew what was happening, of course! Someone had come to steal his mother's hens! The hens across the road had been taken – the hens two houses away had all been stolen the week before – and now the thieves were here to take his own mother's hens – the hens she was so proud of, that laid so well. Why, they each had their own name and would come running when they were called!

Thomas stood there, as still as could be. He didn't think of running away. He just thought of his mother's face if she heard next day that all her precious hens had been stolen in the night. She would be very sad indeed.

But what could he *do*? There wasn't time to go back to the house and warn his father – the

hens would have been taken by then.

And he certainly couldn't fight the men – that would be silly. Thomas simply didn't know *what* to do.

Then he remembered something. He had heard a car stop outside in the lane, just as he had come down the garden to look for Rosebud. That must be the men's car. It was still standing out in the lane – would there be another man in it? Perhaps not. If the car was empty, then – then – Thomas could open the door and take out the key that started the car!

Without the ignition key, the car could not be started. And so the men wouldn't be able to get away!

What a wonderful idea! But would it work? Thomas slid to the other side of the bush, and ran quietly down the grass to the garden gate that led into the lane. He wasn't afraid of the dark any more – how peculiar! He wasn't afraid of bumping into things and hurting himself, either. He just thought of that car, and taking its key.

The car was there, with no lights on at all. Thomas went cautiously to it. There didn't seem to be anyone inside. He quietly opened the door nearest the steering wheel. He put in his hand and groped over the dashboard. He found the key – and he pulled it out! Now the car could not be started!

His heart was beating fast again, but with excitement and triumph now, not with fear. He went back through the gate, hearing the hens

cluck in the house as he did so. The men were even now stuffing the poor things into their sack.

He ran all the way up to the house without stopping. He tore in at the door and raced to the sitting-room where his mother and father were sitting, reading. They were amazed to see Thomas at that time of night, panting and excited.

'Mummy! Daddy! There are men stealing the hens. But they can't get away because I've taken the key of their car. Here it is. Can you telephone the police – because they could easily catch the thieves now!'

His mother simply couldn't believe her ears, and she sat and stared. But in a trice his father was at the telephone. 'Police station, please. Ah – is that Sergeant Harris? I think we've got the hen-thieves here, Sergeant, at Red-Roof House. My boy's taken the key of their car, so they can't get away. If you come now, you can catch the thieves. Yes – yes – he's really got the key – very smart work on his part!'

'*Thomas*!' said his mother, amazed. 'Do you really – oh, *Thomas* – I would never have thought you could do such a thing. Daddy – isn't it marvellous! Oh, Thomas, I'm so proud of you.'

It wasn't long before a police car roared up the lane. Its lights picked out the thieves' car. The two men were in it, desperately feeling in their pockets for the key. They didn't dream that somebody had taken it! The hens were in the seat behind in a sack.

Well, that was the last of those hen-thieves! They were locked up, and couldn't go robbing other people any more. The police were delighted, and they praised Thomas highly.

'He's not only a brave boy, he's a smart one,'

they said. 'You should be proud of him, sir.'

'I am,' said Thomas's father, and gave Thomas a very proud smile indeed.

'There's just one thing I'd love to know,' said his mother, when the police had gone. 'Why are you holding Janet's doll, Thomas dear?'

'Oh goodness – I forgot all about it,' said Thomas, and he put Rosebud down. 'You may think I'm awfully brave and all the rest of it, Mummy – but all that happened really was that I went out to find Janet's doll for her. I would have been too scared to go and get anything of my own – but I couldn't let little Janet go by herself.'

'You remembered what I said, old son,' said Daddy. 'No matter how much of a coward you are, you have to be brave if it's for other people.'

'Yes, I did remember that,' said Thomas. 'And when I got down to the henhouse and heard those men, I thought how sad Mummy would be if her hens were stolen, and I didn't feel afraid any more. It's easy to be brave for other people, isn't it?'

'Not so very easy!' said Daddy. 'And now, Thomas, you will find out a very strange thing about yourself.'

'What, Daddy?' asked Thomas.

'You'll find that once having been brave for other people, it's *much* easier to be brave for yourself!' said Daddy. 'You'll see what I mean when you go to the swimming pool tomorrow. You'll see the cold water, and think "Pooh! If I can tackle hen-thieves in the middle of the night, what's a bit of cold water?" And you'll jump straight in!'

Daddy was perfectly right, Thomas did jump straight in. He knew he could be brave, because he had *been* brave the night before – and so it was easy to be brave again.

Did you know that? It's really worth remembering.

THE STRANGE
CHRISTMAS TREE

Once upon a time there was a Christmas tree that had been planted by a pixie. But before the tree had grown more than an inch or two high the pixie had gone away – so the tree grew in the wood all by itself, and didn't even know that it was a Christmas tree, for it had never been used at Christmas time at all.

But one Christmas a woodman came by and saw the tree, which had now grown into a fine big one. The man stopped and took his spade from his shoulder.

'I could dig that tree up and sell it for a Christmas tree,' he thought. 'It would fetch a few pounds at least! I'll take it to market tomorrow.'

So he dug it up, put it into a great pot, and staggered to market with it.

And to the market came a mother and her

three children. They saw the tree, and the children shouted in delight.

'Mother! Buy this tree! It's the biggest and the best one here.'

So the mother bought the tree, and the wood-man carried it home for her.

The tree was astonished. What in the world was happening to it? It knew the fairy folk very well indeed, for it had lived with them for years, and knew their gentle ways and little high voices. But this world was something quite different – the people were big and tall, not like the fairy folk – and, how strange, they took trees into their houses and stood them there!

The Christmas tree didn't know about Christmas time. It stood in a corner of a big room in its pot, wondering what would happen next.

The children's mother came in with boxes of toys and ornaments and candles. Soon she had hung dozens of them on the tree, and it began to sparkle and shine as if it were a magic thing. It caught sight of itself in the mirror, and how astonished it was!

'I am beautiful!' said the tree. 'I glitter and shine. I am hung with the most beautiful things! Oh, I like living in this land, and being dressed up like this. I shall have a lovely time here!'

Now the children's mother had told them

they must not even peep into the room where she had put the lovely Christmas tree. But, alas! They were disobedient children, and they meant to see the tree as soon as their mother had gone out.

So that night they all three slipped into the room to see the tree.

'It looks nice,' said Doris.

'It's not so big as the one last year,' said George.

'It hasn't got enough toys on,' said Kenneth.

'There's something *I* mean to get, anyway!' said Doris, pointing to a box of crackers. 'So don't you ask for that, boys!'

'Don't be mean, Doris,' said George. 'You got the crackers last year. It's my turn!'

'Well, I'm going to have the soldiers,' said

Kenneth, and he took hold of a box of them. 'There's only one box this year, George, and as I'm the oldest I'm going to have them. See?'

'Don't be so mean and horrid!' said George.

'Look! Look!' said Doris suddenly. 'Here's a box of chocolates. Shall we undo the lid and take some? Nobody will know.'

Now wasn't that a horrid, mean thing to do? Children who do things like that don't deserve a lovely Christmas tree, and that's just what the tree thought. But it stood there quite still and silent, listening and looking.

The children took the chocolates – but Doris had the biggest one, so they began to quarrel again. George hit Doris, and then Doris smacked Kenneth, and soon they were all fighting. The tree had never seen such behaviour before.

The children bumped against the tree and knocked off a lovely pink glass ornament. It

fell to the floor and broke.

'Silly tree!' said Doris rudely. 'Why can't you hold things properly? Why aren't you as big as last year's tree? You're not half so pretty!'

'Christmas trees are babyish things,' said Kenneth. 'I vote we ask for a bran-tub next year.'

'Yes – who wants a silly old tree now?' said George. 'We're getting too big.'

Then a noise was heard in the hall outside and the children fled, for it was their mother coming home. The tree was left alone, sad and angry. What dreadful children! How it hated staying in their house! But where could it go? It did not know its way back to the wood.

And then the tree saw four little faces pressed against the window, looking in, and heard whispering voices. It was the children of the poor woman down the lane. They had never had a Christmas tree in their lives, and nobody ever gave them Christmas presents, not even their mother, who was far too poor to give them even an orange each.

So the children had come to look at the Christmas tree in the big house.

'It's the most beautiful thing in the world!' said Ida.

'If only I could see all its candles alight and shining I would always be happy when I remembered it,' said Lucy.

'Wouldn't Mother love that box of chocolates,' said Harry.

'I wouldn't want any of those toys for myself,' said Fred. 'I'd just be happy cutting them off the tree and giving them to Mother and to you others.'

The tree listened in surprise and delight. What different children these were. If only it was in *their* home.

Then there came the noise of an opening door and the tree heard George's angry voice: 'There are some children peeping in our windows at our Christmas tree. Go away, you bad, naughty children. You're not to look at our tree!'

The four children ran off at once, afraid. The tree felt angrier than ever. It shivered from top to toe at the thought of that horrid, unkind little boy! It stood there, wishing and wishing that it could leave the house.

And then suddenly it remembered some magic it had learnt from the fairy folk, and it murmured the words to itself. Its roots loosened in the pot. One big one put itself outside – and then another and another – and do you know, in a few moments, that strange Christmas tree was walking on its roots round the room! How strange it looked!

The door was open and the tree went out. The front door was shut, but the garden door

was open for the cat to come in. The tree walked out of it just as the cat came in. The cat gave a scared mew and fled outside again. It wasn't used to trees walking out of a house!

The tree walked down the path and out of the gate. It saw the four children away in the distance, running to their home, in the moonlight. Slowly and softly the Christmas tree followed them. But when it got to their house the door was shut!

The tree didn't mind at all. It preferred to wait in the garden, because its roots liked the feel of the earth.

There was no front garden but there was a small one at the back. So the tree walked round and stood there in the middle. It squeezed its root-feet into the soil and held itself there firmly, a marvellous sight with all its beautiful toys and ornaments and candles.

Then it called to the fairy folk, and they came in wonder. 'Light my candles for me,' rustled the tree, 'and then knock on the children's window.'

So the little folk lit all the candles and then rapped loudly on the children's window. Harry pulled back the curtain – and there was the tree standing in the little back garden, lighted from top to toe, shining softly and beautifully, sparkling and glittering in a wonderful way.

'Look!' shouted Harry. 'Look!' And all the other children crowded to the window, with their mother behind them.

'A Christmas tree for us in our own garden!' shouted Lucy. 'Oh, it's like the one we saw in the big house.'

Harry ran out and shouted to the others in surprise. 'It's *growing* in the ground – it's really growing! It must be magic!'

Everyone crowded round it. The tree was very happy, and glowed brightly. The children gently touched the toys. Harry cut off the box of chocolates and gave it to his mother.

And then Fred cut off the toys and pressed them into everybody's hands. He didn't want any for himself – he was so pleased to be able to give them to those he loved! But Harry made him have the box of soldiers and the red train.

Then they all went indoors out of the cold and left the Christmas tree by itself, still with its candles burning brightly. And that night the fairy folk took it back to its old place in the wood, where it grows to this day, remembering every Christmas time how once it wore candles and ornaments and toys.

As for Doris and George and Kenneth, what do you suppose they thought when they went to have their Christmas tree and found it was gone? Only the big pot was left, and nothing else at all! How they cried! How they sobbed! But I can't help being glad that the tree walked off to the children down the lane!